Science

No part of this publication may be reproduced in whole or in part, or stored in a retrieval system, or transmitted in any form or by any means, electronic, mechanical, photocopying, recording, or otherwise, without written permission of the publisher.

Published by Scholastic Inc., 90 Old Sherman Turnpike, Danbury, CT 06816

SCHOLASTIC and associated logos are trademarks and/or registered trademarks of Scholastic Inc.

ISBN 0-7172-9870-1

Printed in the U.S.A.

First Scholastic Printing, August 2006

Diego's
Sea Turtle Adventure

by
Christine Ricci

illustrated by
Alex Maher

SCHOLASTIC INC.

New York Toronto London Auckland Sydney
Mexico City New Delhi Hong Kong Buenos Aires

"Help! Help! ¡Ayúdenme!" Diego heard as his hang glider sailed over the rainforest canopy. "That sounds like an animal in trouble!" he thought. "I've got to find out what animal needs help!" Diego glided toward the Animal Rescue Center.

Diego's sister, Alicia, met him on the Science Deck.

Their special camera, Click, located the animal in trouble.

"What kind of animal is it?" asked Alicia.

"It's a sea turtle!" Diego exclaimed. "And not just any sea turtle. It's our friend, Luis, the Hawksbill Sea Turtle!"

Luis was stranded in the middle of a busy harbor.

"We've got to rescue Luis before a boat bumps into him. *¡Al rescate!* To the rescue!" Diego called out as he set out in the direction of the ocean.

"Go, Diego, go!" cheered Alicia.

Diego was almost to the ocean when he heard a loud rumble. "Whoa!" shouted Diego as sand slid off the dunes, blocking his path.

10

"Bobos! Bobos!" giggled two voices from the top of the dunes. The Bobo Brothers were making sand slide down the side of the dunes. Diego had to stop them.

"Freeze, Bobos!" he yelled.

The Bobo Brothers froze. "Oops! Sorry, Diego," they called as they ran off.

"Hawksbill sea turtles have brown shells with yellow stripes and sharp pointy beaks," Diego said as he pulled out his Spotting Scope and scanned the harbor. Finally, he spotted Luis, the Hawksbill Sea Turtle!

Luis was drifting close to several large boats. "Oh, no!" cried Diego. "A boat could bump into Luis!"

To rescue Luis, Diego needed something to ride across the water. "Rescue Pack can transform into anything I need. ¡*Actívate!*" shouted Diego.

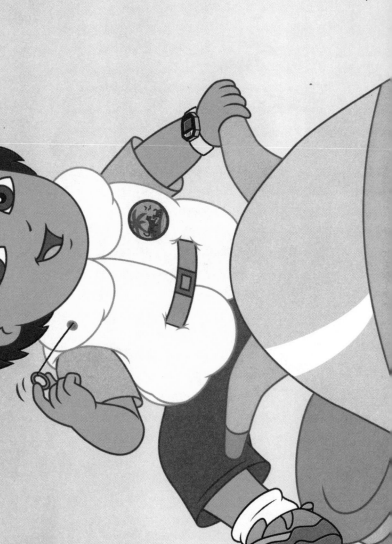

Rescue Pack transformed into a jet ski. Diego pulled a cord on his vest and it turned into a life vest. Then, Diego jumped onto the jet ski and sped toward the busy harbor.

When he got close, he drove in a large circle around Luis, dropping warning flags in the water so that the other boats would see them.

"Luis, are you OK?" asked Diego.

"I'm OK!" replied Luis. "But I can't find my way home."

"I can help you," said Diego as he pushed a button on his jet ski. A special Rescue Board popped out and slid into the water. "Hop on!" called Diego. "I'll tow you to safety!"

With Luis on the Rescue Board, Diego had to find a way out of the harbor. Suddenly, he heard a beeping sound.

"That's my Video Watch. It's my sister, Alicia, calling from the Animal Rescue Center," he explained to Luis.

"Diego, the harbor is filled with fishing nets. You could get stuck," warned Alicia. "To get out of the harbor, follow the red buoys from numbers one to five."

"OK, Alicia," replied Diego. "Thanks!"

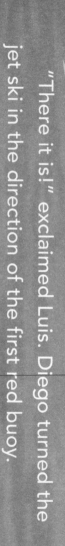

"I need to follow the red buoy," said Diego. "Do you see red buoy number one?"

"There it is!" exclaimed Luis. Diego turned the jet ski in the direction of the first red buoy.

"Uno . . . dos . . . tres . . . cuatro . . . cinco," counted Diego as he jet skied past all of the red buoys toward the ocean.

Once they were out in the ocean, Diego needed to help Luis find his home. "I live near a beautiful reef with other hawksbill sea turtles," said Luis.

One reef they found was filled with large turtles with black and white shells. "Those are leatherback sea turtles," said Luis.

"We need to find a reef filled with turtles with sharp, pointy beaks. Do you see it?" asked Diego.

"There it is!" cheered Luis. "That's my home!"

Diego helped Luis gently slide off the Rescue Board and into the ocean water. All of the hawksbill sea turtles swam over to Luis. They were very happy that Luis was back home on their reef.

Luis was especially glad to be home. He smiled up at Diego and said, "Thanks for helping me. *¡Gracias!*"

Diego waved goodbye to Luis. *"¡Misión cumplida!
Rescue complete!"* cheered Diego. "That was a
great animal adventure!"

Nick Jr. Play-to-Learn™ Fundamentals

Skills every child needs, in stories every child will love!

colors + shapes	Recognizing and identifying basic shapes and colors in the context of a story.
emotions	Learning to identify and understand a wide range of emotions, such as happy, sad, and excited.
imagination	Fostering creative thinking skills through role-play and make-believe.
123 math	Recognizing early math in the world around us, such as patterns, shapes, numbers, and sequences.
music + movement	Celebrating the sounds and rhythms of music and dance.
physical	Building coordination and confidence through physical activity and play.
problem solving	Using critical thinking skills, such as observing, listening, and following directions, to make predictions and solve problems.
reading + language	Developing a lifelong love of reading through high interest stories and characters.
science	Fostering curiosity and an interest in the natural world around us.
social skills + cultural diversity	Developing respect for others as unique, interesting people.

Science

Conversation Spark

Questions and activities for play-to-learn parenting.

Luis helped Diego learn the difference between hawksbill sea turtles and leatherback sea turtles. What is the same about the two kinds of turtles? What is different? Can you draw the different kinds of turtles?

ENGLISH/SPANISH GLOSSARY and PRONUNCIATION GUIDE

ENGLISH	SPANISH	PRONUNCIATION
Help	Ayúdenme	ah-YOO-den-meh
To the rescue	Al rescate	al res-CAH-teh
Activate	Actívate	ahk-TEE-vah-tay
One	Uno	OO-noh
Two	Dos	DOHS
Three	Tres	TREHS
Four	Cuatro	KWAH-troh
Five	Cinco	SEEN-koh
Thank you	Gracias	GRAH-see-ahs
Rescue Complete	Misión Cumplida	mee-see-OHN coom-PLEE-dah